E
ALÉ

# NADIA THE WILLFUL

by Sue Alexander
pictures by Lloyd Bloom

PANTHEON BOOKS

Text copyright © 1983 by Sue Alexander
Illustrations copyright © 1983 by Lloyd Bloom
All rights reserved under International and Pan-American
Copyright Conventions. Published in the United States by Pantheon Books,
a division of Random House, Inc., New York, and simultaneously
in Canada by Random House of Canada Limited, Toronto.
Manufactured in the United States of America
1   3   5   7   9   10   8   6   4   2
First Edition

Library of Congress Cataloging in Publication Data

Alexander, Sue, 1933- Nadia the Willful.

Summary: When her favorite brother disappears in the desert forever,
Nadia refuses to let him be forgotten, despite her father's bitter decree
that his name shall not be uttered.
[1. Arabs—Fiction.   2. Death—Fiction.   3. Brothers and sisters—
Fiction]   I. Bloom, Lloyd, ill.   II. Title.
PZ7.A3784Nad   1983   [E]   82-12602
ISBN 0-394-85265-6
ISBN 0-394-95265-0 (lib. bdg.)

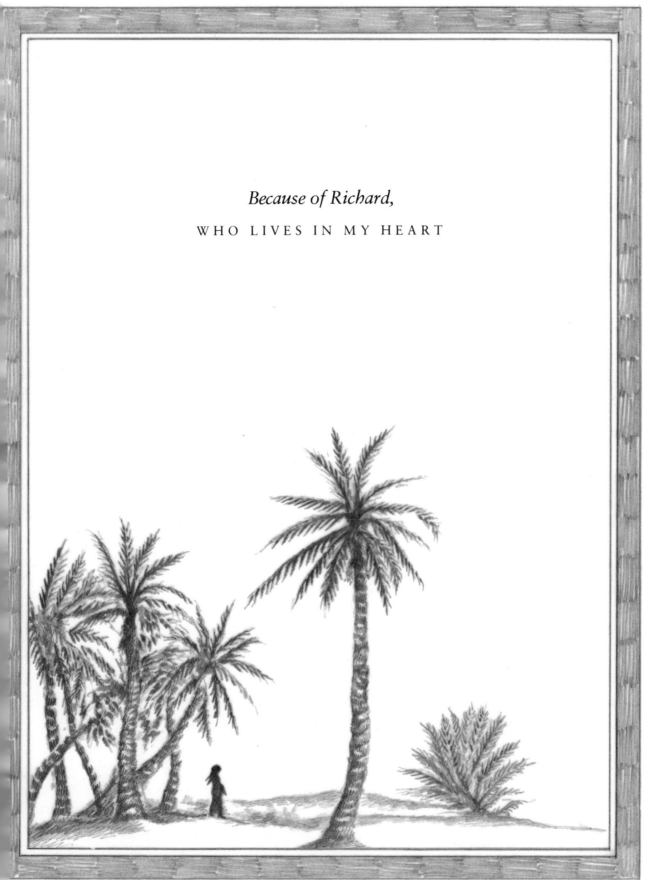

*Because of Richard,*

WHO LIVES IN MY HEART

where the Bedouin move their tents to follow the fertile grasses, there lived a girl whose stubbornness and flashing temper caused her to be known throughout the desert as Nadia the Willful.

Nadia's father, the sheik Tarik, whose kindness and graciousness caused his name to be praised in every tent, did not know what to do with his willful daughter.

Only Hamed, the eldest of Nadia's six brothers and Tarik's favorite son, could calm Nadia's temper when it flashed. "Oh, angry one," he would say, "shall we see how long you can stay that way?" And he would laugh and tease and pull at her dark hair until she laughed back. Then she would follow Hamed wherever he led.

One day before dawn, Hamed mounted his father's great white stallion and rode to the west to seek new grazing ground for the sheep. Nadia stood with her father at the edge of the oasis and watched him go.

Hamed did not return.

Nadia rode behind her father as he traveled across the desert from oasis to oasis, seeking Hamed.

Shepherds told them of seeing a great white stallion fleeing before the pillars of wind that stirred the sand. And they said that the horse carried no rider.

Passing merchants, their camels laden with spices and sweets for the bazaar, told of the emptiness of the desert they had crossed.

Tribesmen, strangers, everyone whom Tarik asked, sighed and gazed into the desert, saying, "Such is the will of Allah."

At last Tarik knew in his heart that his favorite son, Hamed, had been claimed, as other Bedouin before him, by the drifting sands. And he told Nadia what he knew—that Hamed was dead.

Nadia screamed and wept and stamped the sand, crying, "Not even Allah will take Hamed from me!" until her father could bear no more and sternly bade her to silence.

Nadia's grief knew no bounds. She walked blindly through the oasis neither seeing nor hearing those who would console her. And Tarik was silent. For days he sat inside his tent, speaking not at all and barely tasting the meals set before him.

Then, on the seventh day, Tarik came out of his tent. He called all his people to him, and when they were assembled, he spoke. "From this day forward," he said, "let no one utter Hamed's name. Punishment shall be swift for those who would remind me of what I have lost."

Hamed's mother wept at the decree. The people of the clan looked at one another uneasily. All could see the hardness that had settled on the sheik's face and the coldness in his eyes, and so they said nothing. But they obeyed.

Nadia, too, did as her father decreed, though each day held something to remind her of Hamed. As she passed her brothers at play she remembered games Hamed had taught her. As she walked by the women weaving patches for the tents, and heard them talking and laughing, she remembered tales Hamed had told her and how they had made her laugh. And as she watched the shepherds with their flock she remembered the little black lamb Hamed had loved.

Each memory brought Hamed's name to Nadia's lips, but she stilled the sound. And each time that she did so, her unhappiness grew until, finally, she could no longer contain it. She wept and raged at anyone and anything that crossed her path. Soon everyone at the oasis fled at her approach. And she was more lonely than she had ever been before.

One day, as Nadia passed the place where her brothers were playing, she stopped to watch them. They were playing one of the games that Hamed had taught her. But they were playing it wrong.

Without thinking, Nadia called out to them. "That is not the way! Hamed said that first you jump this way and then you jump back!"

Her brothers stopped their game and looked around in fear. Had Tarik heard Nadia say Hamed's name? But the sheik was nowhere to be seen.

"Teach us, Nadia, as our brother taught you," said her smallest brother.

And so she did. Then she told them of other games and how Hamed had taught her to play them. And as she spoke of Hamed she felt an easing of the hurt within her.

So she went on speaking of him.

She went to where the women sat at their loom and spoke of
Hamed. She told them tales that Hamed had told her. And she
told how he had made her laugh as he was telling them.

At first the women were afraid to listen to the willful girl and
covered their ears, but after a time, they listened and laughed
with her.

"Remember your father's promise of punishment!" Nadia's mother warned when she heard Nadia speaking of Hamed. "Cease, I implore you!"

Nadia knew that her mother had reason to be afraid, for Tarik, in his grief and bitterness, had grown quick-tempered and sharp of tongue. But she did not know how to tell her mother that speaking of Hamed eased the pain she felt, and so she said only, "I will speak of my brother! I will!" And she ran away from the sound of her mother's voice.

She went to where the shepherds tended the flock and spoke
of Hamed. The shepherds ran from her in fear and hid behind
the sheep. But Nadia went on speaking. She told of Hamed's

love for the little black lamb and how he had taught it to leap at his whistle. Soon the shepherds left off their hiding and came to listen. Then they told their own stories of Hamed and the little black lamb.

The more Nadia spoke of Hamed, the clearer his face became
in her mind. She could see his smile and the light in his eyes. She
could hear his voice. And the clearer Hamed's voice and face
became, the less Nadia hurt inside and the less her temper flashed.
At last, she was filled with peace.

But her mother was still afraid for her willful daughter. Again and again she sought to quiet Nadia so that Tarik's bitterness would not be turned against her. And again and again Nadia tossed her head and went on speaking of Hamed.

Soon, all who listened could see Hamed's face clearly before them.

One day, the youngest shepherd came to Nadia's tent calling, "Come, Nadia! See Hamed's black lamb, it has grown so big and strong!"

But it was not Nadia who came out of the tent.

It was Tarik.

On the sheik's face was a look more fierce than that of a desert hawk, and when he spoke, his words were as sharp as a scimitar.

"I have forbidden my son's name to be said. And I promised punishment to whoever disobeyed my command. So shall it be. Before the sun sets and the moon casts its first shadow on the sand, you will be gone from this oasis—never to return."

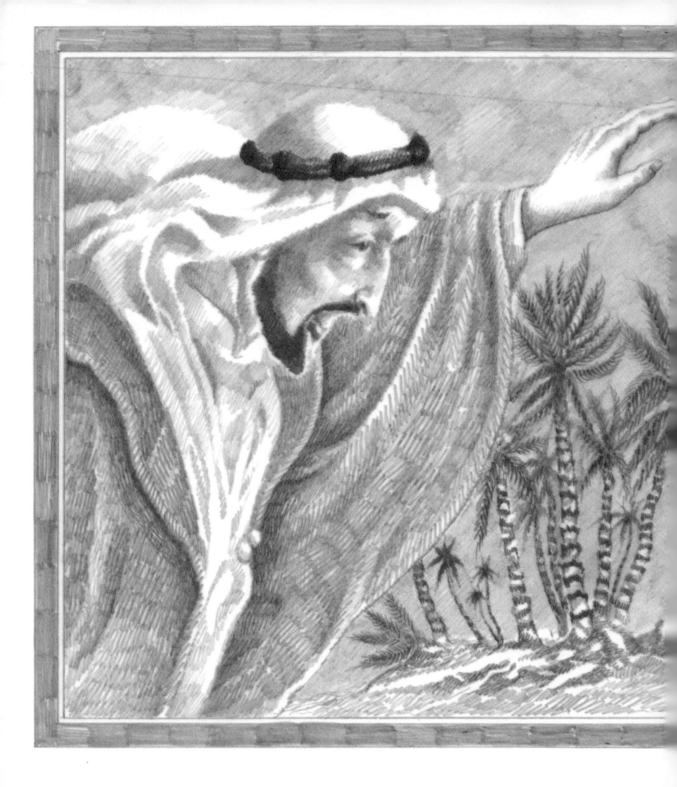

"No!" cried Nadia, hearing her father's words.

"I have spoken!" roared the sheik. "It shall be done!"

Trembling, the shepherd went to gather his possessions.
And the rest of the clan looked at one another uneasily and
muttered among themselves.

In the hours that followed, fear of being banished to the desert made everyone turn away from Nadia as she tried to tell them of Hamed and the things he had done and said.

And the less she was listened to, the less she was able to recall Hamed's face and voice. And the less she recalled, the more her temper raged within her, destroying the peace she had found.

By evening, she could stand it no longer. She went to where her father sat, staring into the desert, and stood before him.

"You will not rob me of my brother Hamed!" she cried, stamping her foot. "I will not let you!"

Tarik looked at her, his eyes colder than the desert night.

But before he could utter a word, Nadia spoke again. "Can you recall Hamed's face? Can you still hear his voice?"

Tarik started in surprise, and his answer seemed to come unbidden to his lips. "No, I cannot! Day after day I have sat in this spot where I last saw Hamed, trying to remember the look, the sound, the happiness that was my beloved son—but I cannot."

And he wept.

Nadia's tone became gentle. "There is a way, honored father," she said. "Listen."

And she began to speak of Hamed. She told of walks she and Hamed had taken, and of talks they had had. She told how he had taught her games, told her tales and calmed her when she was angry. She told many things that she remembered, some happy and some sad.

And when she was done with the telling, she said gently, "Can you not recall him now, Father? Can you not see his face? Can you not hear his voice?"

Tarik nodded through his tears, and for the first time since Hamed had been gone, he smiled.

"Now you see," Nadia said, her tone more gentle than the softest of the desert breezes, "there is a way that Hamed can be with us still."

The sheik pondered what Nadia had said. After a long time, he spoke, and the sharpness was gone from his voice.

"Tell my people to come before me, Nadia," he said. "I have something to say to them."

When all were assembled, Tarik said, "From this day forward,
let my daughter Nadia be known not as Willful, but as Wise.
And let her name be praised in every tent, for she has given me
back my beloved son."

And so it was. The shepherd returned to his flock, kindness and graciousness returned to the oasis, and Nadia's name was praised in every tent. And Hamed lived again—in the hearts of all who remembered him.

SUE ALEXANDER is the author of many highly praised books for children, including the *Witch, Goblin, and Ghost I Am Reading* books, three collections of plays, and *Finding Your First Job*—the 1980 Golden Kite Honor Book for Non-Fiction. She is on the board of directors of the Society of Children's Book Writers, and is a recipient of the Dorothy C. McKenzie Award for a distinguished contribution to the field of children's literature. She has three grown children, and lives with her husband in Canoga Park, California. *Nadia The Willful* grew out of her own experience of loss and remembrance.

LLOYD BLOOM was born in New York City. He graduated with honors from Hunter College and received an M.F.A. in painting from Indiana University. He also studied at the Art Students League and at the New School for Social Research with Uri Shulevitz in a workshop for picture book writing and illustration. His work has been shown at the Society of Illustrators, and he has illustrated many books for children including *We Be Warm Till Springtime Comes, The Green Book,* and *Arthur, For the Very First Time,* the winner of the Golden Kite Award. Mr. Bloom now lives in Brooklyn, New York.